The Berenstain Bears

SAY PLEASE and Thank You

by Jan & Mike Berenstain

HARPER

An Imprint of HarperCollinsPublishers

The Berenstain Bears Say Please and Thank You   Copyright © 2011 by Berenstain Bears, Inc.   All rights reserved. Manufactured in China.   No part of this book may be used or reproduced in any manner whatsoever without written permission except in the case of brief quotations embodied in critical articles and reviews. For information address HarperCollins Children's Books, a division of HarperCollins Publishers, 10 East 53rd Street, New York, NY 10022.   www.harpercollinschildrens.com
Library of Congress Cataloging-in-Publication Data is available.
ISBN 978-0-06-057437-6 (trade bdg.) — ISBN 978-0-06-057438-3 (lib. bdg.)
Typography by Kirsten Berger   11 12 13 14 15 SCP 10 9 8 7 6 5 4 3 2 1   ❖   First Edition

PLEASE!

Brother and Papa Bear were going fishing. They had their rods and reels. They had their hooks and bobbers. Most important, they had their bait—a nice can of worms.

Down by the pond, they baited their hooks and cast out their lines. Brother watched his bobber bob up and down in the breeze. But it didn't go underwater. If a fish bit, it would go all the way under.

It was quiet by the pond and Papa fell asleep. All you could hear was his snoring. Then Brother's bobber bobbed up and down. It went all the way under the water.

"I've got a bite!" said Brother. "Huh?" said Papa, waking up. "Don't pull too hard. Just give it a little yank and reel it in."

Brother landed a fine fat sunfish. They took out the hook and let it go. It wriggled away under the lily pads.

"That was fun!" said Brother, getting ready to bait his hook again. "Pass the worms."

"Aren't you forgetting something, Brother?" asked Papa.

Brother was puzzled. "I've got my rod and reel," he said.

"Right," said Papa.

"I've got my hook and bobber," said Brother.

"Uh-huh," said Papa.

"I just need another worm," said Brother. "What am I forgetting?"

"You forgot to say 'Please!'" Papa told him.

"Oh, yeah!" said Brother. "I was so excited about catching the fish that I forgot. Will you please pass the worms?" he added.

"Of course." Papa smiled, passing him the can of worms.

Brother baited his hook and cast out his line.

"It's always important to remember to be polite," said Papa, "even when you're going fishing."

"Will it help us catch more fish?" asked Brother, watching his bobber.

"Maybe not," admitted Papa. "But it makes everything go smoother." And he settled back to finish his nap.

THANK YOU!

One afternoon, Brother, Sister, and Honey Bear were making mud pies. They made apple mud pies, cherry mud pies, blueberry mud pies, and coconut cream mud pies.

"If we sell these pies," said Sister, "we can make a lot of money."

"Good idea," said Brother.

"Good!" said Honey.

They put their mud pies by the side of the road with a sign: FRESH-BAKED MUD PIES—5¢.

Too-Tall Grizzly and his gang came along.

"Why would we want to buy your stupid mud pies?" Too-Tall laughed and his gang laughed, too.

Queenie McBear and her friends rode by on their bikes. "We can't eat mud," said Queenie. "Come, girls!" They pedaled off in a cloud of dust.

Brother's and Sister's friends walked past. "These are nice mud pies," they said. "But we don't have any money." They walked on.

"No one wants our mud pies." Brother sighed.

"We'll wait until the right customer comes along," said Sister.

At last, a long lavender limousine pulled up, and Mayor and Mrs. Honeypot got out.

"Oh, isn't this darling!" said Mrs. Honeypot. "You cubs are so creative. I'll buy every one of your pies!"

Sister, Brother, and Honey didn't know what to say.

"Shouldn't you say something now?"
Mrs. Honeypot smiled.

"Th-th-thank you!" said Sister.

"Thank you!" said Brother.

"Thanks!" said Honey.

"That's the right thing to say
when someone buys all your mud
pies." Mrs. Honeypot laughed.
"Come, Horace."

So Mrs. Honeypot bought all their mud pies for five cents
apiece and drove off with them in the long lavender limousine.

"Wow!" said Sister as the cubs counted their money. "She
must really like pie."

YOU'RE WELCOME!

The Bear family was down at the beach for the day. They went swimming, buried each other in the sand, played Frisbee, and lay in the sun. After lying in the sun for about five minutes, Sister, Brother, and Honey felt too hot.

"Let's build a sand castle," said Sister.

Brother and Honey liked the idea. They started to pile up sand.

"Building a sand castle, I see," said Papa. "I'll help. I'm a sand castle expert."

Papa helped the cubs make a huge sand pile.

"Now we'll need driftwood, shells, and buckets of water," said Papa.

Brother found pieces of driftwood, Sister collected shells, and Honey found a long seagull feather. Papa carried buckets of water from the sea.

First they built a tower and wetted it down with seawater to make it stick together. They decorated it with shells and put the seagull feather in the top for a flag.

Next they made a
wall and a moat with a
driftwood drawbridge.
They dug a trench
down to the water to
fill it up.

"This is the best sand
castle ever!" said Sister.

"Thanks for helping
us, Papa," said Brother. "We
couldn't have done it without you."

"You're welcome!" said Papa. "I love to
build things with you. You're very welcome, indeed!"

Just then a big wave came rolling up the beach. The cubs ran away, but the
wave crashed over the sand castle. It crashed over Papa, too.

The cubs helped Papa up.

"Thanks!" said Papa.

"You're welcome!" said Brother and Sister.

"Welcome!" said Honey.

Their sand castle was washed away. The only thing left was the seagull feather sticking in the sand.

"Let's build another one," said Sister.

"Okay!" said Brother.

"Kay!" said Honey.

"I'll help you," said Papa.

"Thanks, Papa!" said the cubs, giving him a big hug.

"You're welcome!" said Papa Bear.

EXCUSE ME!

Brother, Sister, and Honey were playing pirates in the backyard. The picnic table was their pirate ship. A beach umbrella was their sail. They had long balloons for pirate swords. Mama's black bathing suit was a pirate flag. "ARRR!" cried Brother. He was Captain Cub. "This desert island looks like a good place to bury our treasure." He pointed to the birdhouse. "Drop anchor!"

Their treasure chest was a box of old comic books. They carried it to the birdhouse to bury it.

"ARRR!" someone else cried. It was Too-Tall Grizzly and his gang. "I'm Black Bruin, the King of the Pirates. Hand over that treasure!"

"Curse you, Black Bruin!" said Brother.

Too-Tall laughed and his gang laughed, too.

"You will stay on this island until you rot!" said Too-Tall.

"Marooned!" said Sister.
"Who are you calling a 'maroon'?" asked Brother.
"That just means we're stuck here," said Sister.

Too-Tall and his gang took over the picnic table ship and opened the treasure chest.
"Oh, boy!" said Too-Tall. "Comic books!"
They started to read. Brother, Sister, and Honey decided they didn't like being marooned.

"Excuse me!" said Brother.
"Yes?" said Too-Tall.
"May we join you?" asked Brother.
"Sure," said Too-Tall. "Come aboard."
Brother, Sister, and Honey joined Too-Tall
on the picnic table to read comic books.

"It's lucky you said 'Excuse me!'"
said Too-Tall, "or I wouldn't
have let you come aboard."
"It always pays to be
polite," said Sister, "if
you're marooned."

I'M SORRY!

It was a snowy day in Bear Country. Brother, Sister, Honey, and their friends were having fun in the snow. First they made a snowman. They rolled up a big ball of snow. They rolled it and rolled it and rolled it. It was huge.

"Great!" said Sister. "That can be the head. Now let's make the body."

But Brother had other ideas. "Let's have a snowball fight instead," he said.

"Okay!" said Cousin Fred. "First we need snow forts."

The cubs set to work building two snow forts. The big ball of snow was part of one.

Then the cubs made snowballs and piled them up inside the forts.

"Ready?" Brother called to Fred.

"Ready!" Fred called back.

"Go!" yelled Brother, and the snowballs began to fly. The cubs were safe inside their forts. None of the snowballs hit them.

"We can't win this way," said Sister. "We need to attack."

Brother, Sister, and Honey grabbed snowballs and ran out of their fort.

"YAAAH!" they yelled.

A big snowball came sailing over and hit Sister right in the face, "SPLAT!"

"I'm sorry!" said Cousin Fred. "I didn't mean to hit you in the face."

"Don't worry," said Sister. "Just hearing you say 'I'm sorry' makes me feel better."

She picked up a snowball. "And this makes me feel even better!" She threw the snowball at Fred.

"I'm sorry!" She laughed and the snowball fight went on. When they ran out of snowballs, they all went inside for hot chocolate. It was delicious.

HOW ARE YOU?

One bright spring day, Brother and Sister met their friends down at the playground.

"Hi, Lizzy!" said Sister. "How are you?"

"I'm fine, thanks," said Lizzy. "How about you?"

"I'm great!" said Sister. "Come on, let's go on the slides."

Sister and Lizzy raced each other to the slides. Sister got there first. They took turns going down. Then they headed for the whirligig.

All the cubs climbed
on the whirligig and held
on tight. Brother and
Cousin Fred pushed it
around and around, faster
and faster.

"WHEEE!" they all cried.

The whirligig slowed down and came to a stop.
The cubs climbed off. But Lizzy could hardly stand up.

"How are you, Lizzy?" asked Sister. "You look a little green."

"I'm not sure how I am," said Lizzy. "I feel dizzy! How are you, Sister?"

"I'm fine," said Sister. "But I'm worried about you."

"That's nice of you," said Lizzy. "But I'll be okay. I feel better already."

"Good!" said Sister. "Come on, let's go on the monkey bars."

So Sister and Lizzy climbed on the monkey bars like the two little monkeys they are.

NICE TO MEET YOU!

On the first day of school, Brother and Sister were waiting at the bus stop when Cousin Fred came up. A new cub was with him.

"Brother and Sister," he said, "I'd like to introduce you to my new neighbor, Bobby Brown. He just moved from Big Bear City."

"Nice to meet you!" said Sister, shaking hands. Brother did the same.

"It's nice to meet you, too!" said Bobby. "I'm glad everyone here is so friendly."

"Well," said Brother, "maybe not everyone."

That's when Too-Tall Grizzly and his gang showed up.

"A new cub!" said Too-Tall. "Let's have some fun!"

But Brother and Sister stood in the way.

"Leave Bobby alone!" said Sister. "He's not bothering you."

"Oh, the new cub has some new friends!" said Too-Tall. "How sweet!" Too-Tall laughed and his gang laughed, too.

Soon the bus pulled up to take them to school.

Later, in gym class, the cubs were all playing soccer. Too-Tall got the ball and took it down the field. But Bobby Brown stole it and scored a goal instead.

"Wow!" said Brother. "That Bobby Brown sure can play."

Too-Tall came up to Bobby, frowning.

"Uh-oh!" said Sister. "What's going to happen?"

But Too-Tall just stuck out his hand.

"Nice to meet you!" said Too-Tall. "You're quite a soccer player."

"Nice to meet you, too, Too-Tall!" said Bobby, shaking hands.

"Okay," said Too-Tall. "Enough of the polite stuff. Let's play some soccer!"

LET ME HELP!

Bear Country School was getting ready for the school play, *The Music Bear*. Teacher Bob was in charge in the school auditorium.

"Okay," said Teacher Bob. "Everyone trying out for a part—over here! Everyone working on scenery—over here!"

It was a lot of work to put on the school play. But it was a lot of fun, too. Brother and Sister wanted to work on the scenery.

The Music Bear had a lot of scenery. There were houses and trees, living rooms and staircases, a railway station, and even a whole city park. Brother and Sister started painting a tree. Teacher Bob was painting a big backdrop of the park all by himself.

"Let me help!" said Brother.

"Me, too!" said Sister.

"Okay, Brother and Sister," said Teacher Bob.

They painted and painted. When they were done, it looked just like a real park.

"A job well done!" said Teacher Bob. "Thanks for helping, Brother and Sister."

"You're welcome, Teacher Bob," they said. "We like to help."

Soon all the sets were finished and it was time for opening night.

The curtain went up and the show began. There was singing and dancing, a parade down Main Street, and, of course, all those beautiful sets. Sister and Brother were proud of their work. When the show was over, everyone clapped and clapped and clapped.

"Let me help!" said Sister, clapping, too.

"And me!" said Brother, joining in.

"*And me!*" said Teacher Bob, whistling between his fingers.

With everyone's help, *The Music Bear* was a big hit.